The Tiara Club

at Pearl Palace

D0995667

y

For my friends in Sri Lanka,
with love and thanks
VF
With special thanks to JD

www.tiaraclub.co.uk

ORCHARD BOOKS
338 Euston Road, London NW1 3BH
Orchard Books Australia
Level 17/207 Kent St, Sydney, NSW 2000
A Paperback Original
First published in 2007 by Orchard Books
Text © Vivian French 2007
Cover illustration © Sarah Gibb 2007
Inside illustrations © Orchard Books 2007

A CIP catalogue record for this book is available
from the British Library.

ISBN 978 1 84616 499 6

1 3 5 7 9 10 8 6 4 2

Printed in Great Britain

The paper and board used in this paperback are natural recyclable
products made from wood grown in sustainable forests.
The manufacturing processes conform to the environmental
regulations of the country of origin.

Orchard Books is a division of Hachette Children's Books,
an Hachette Livre UK company.

www.orchardbooks.co.uk

The Tiara Club

at Pearl Palace

Princess Isabella

and the Snow-White Unicorn

By Vivian French

ORCHARD BOOKS

The Royal Palace Academy
for the Preparation of Perfect Princesses

(Known to our students as "*The Princess Academy*")

OUR SCHOOL MOTTO:
*A Perfect Princess always thinks of others
before herself, and is kind, caring and truthful.*

**Pearl Palace offers a complete education for
Tiara Club princesses with emphasis on the arts
and outdoor activities. The curriculum includes:**

*A special Princess
Sports Day*

*A trip to the Magical
Mountains*

*Preparation for the
Silver Swan Award
(stories and poems)*

*A visit to the King
Rudolfo's Exhibition of
Musical Instruments*

Our headteacher, King Everest, is present at all times,
and students are well looked after by the head fairy
godmother, Fairy G, and her assistant, Fairy Angora.

Our resident staff and visiting experts include:

*QUEEN MOLLY
(Sports and games)*

*LADY MALVEENA
(Secretary to King Everest)*

*LORD HENRY
(Natural History)*

*QUEEN MOTHER MATILDA
(Etiquette, Posture and
Flower Arranging)*

We award tiara points to encourage our Tiara Club princesses towards the next level. All princesses who win enough points at Pearl Palace will be presented with their Pearl Sashes and attend a celebration ball.

Pearl Sash Tiara Club princesses are invited to go on to Emerald Castle, our very special residence for Perfect Princesses, where they may continue their education at a higher level.

PLEASE NOTE:
Pets are not allowed at Pearl Palace.
Princesses are expected to arrive at
the Academy with a *minimum* of:

TWENTY BALLGOWNS
*(with all necessary hoops,
petticoats, etc)*

TWELVE DAY DRESSES

SEVEN GOWNS
*suitable for garden parties,
and other special
day occasions*

TWELVE TIARAS

DANCING SHOES
five pairs

VELVET SLIPPERS
three pairs

RIDING BOOTS
two pairs

*Cloaks, muffs, stoles, gloves
and other essential
accessories as required*

Dear princess - I'm so very pleased
you're here at Pearl Palace with me
and all my friends from Lily Room!
I'm Princess Isabella; I expect you
already know Hannah, Lucy, Grace, Ellie
and Sarah. And have you met the twins,
Diamonde and Gruella? If you have,
you'll know what they're like -
just awful! Especially when we
go out on school trips...

Chapter One

Lessons had finished, and we were in the recreation room playing Snakes and Ladders. I'd just slid down a HUGE ladder, so I didn't mind when Amy from Poppy Room came hurrying through the door and interrupted us.

"I've got news!" she said. "There's a new teacher, and he's

9

dressed all in green and he's going to teach us natural history! His name's Lord Henry and even his SHOES are green!" And she whizzed off again.

"What's natural history?" Ellie asked. "Is it trees and flowers?"

"And animals and birds as well," Sarah told her.

Lucy looked SO excited. "Maybe he'll take us out on amazing trips!"

Hannah's eyes began to sparkle. "Oh – I do hope so!" she said.

"I'll tell you what," Grace suggested, "why don't we go and look at the noticeboard? That'll tell us if anything new has been planned."

"Good idea," I said, and we tidied away our game and hurried off. As we reached the board, Fairy Angora (she's the assistant fairy godmother at the Princess Academy) came towards us holding a piece of paper.

"Good evening, my precious petals," she said. "You've got a wonderful treat at the end of this week. We've got a new teacher here at Pearl Palace, and he's invited all the students to his castle in the Magical Mountains for the weekend."

"WOW!" Lucy went quite pale.

"The Magical Mountains? Isn't that where unicorns are supposed to live?"

Fairy Angora nodded as she pinned the details of the trip up on the board. "That's right, my darling. Of course they hardly ever show themselves, but you never know. You might be lucky!"

"Is that why we're going there?" I asked. "To look for unicorns?"

Fairy Angora shook her head. "Lord Henry is very interested in natural history, and King Everest thought it would be good for you to learn more about the world outside."

"'A Perfect Princess shows an interest in all birds, animals and living things, great or small,'" Lucy quoted. She suddenly looked doubtful. "Does that mean things like slugs as well?"

Fairy Angora laughed. "I don't think we'll be studying slugs."

"WE?" Hannah gave a little

skip. "Does that mean you're coming with us, Fairy Angora?"

"I certainly am, my darlings." Fairy Angora straightened the notice, and walked away.

"Oh – that makes it even better!" Hannah said, and we all nodded in agreement.

"Makes WHAT even better?" asked a sneering voice from behind us. I turned, and saw Diamonde and Gruella.

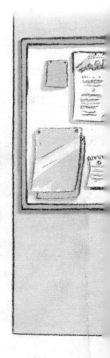

"We're all going to the Magical Mountains!" I said. "Isn't that BRILLIANT?"

"H'm." Diamonde gave me one of her special superior stares. "And I suppose you think you're going to see a unicorn, Isabella."

"You never know," I told her. "I might."

"Mummy says only the most Perfect Princesses ever get to see them." Diamonde tossed her head. "So if ANYONE gets to see them, it's sure to be me and Gruella. So there!"

Chapter Two

We could hardly wait for the weekend to come. Sarah made an hour chart, and we took it in turns to tick off each hour as it passed...but it still seemed AGES until Saturday. When it finally arrived we woke up REALLY early. It was lucky we did, because Fairy Angora knocked on our door not long after.

"Time to get up, petals!" she called, and we were out of bed in no time at all. We'd packed our bags the night before, so by the time Lord Henry strode into the entrance hall we were ready and waiting.

"Good girls! Jolly good show!" he said when he saw us. "The coaches are outside to take us to the station, and the royal train will leave at 8.30 exactly."

"Did you say a TRAIN?" Diamonde screeched. "A TRAIN? Mummy NEVER lets us travel by train. Does she, Gruella?"

Before Gruella could answer
Lord Henry gave a loud laugh.
"Haw! Haw! Super joke, girls!
Super! Into the coach you hop,
now." And he almost pushed
the twins out of the front door.

They were so surprised they didn't say another word.

Lucy grinned at me. "I like Lord Henry!" she whispered.

"Me too!" I whispered back.

The train was fabulous. Our carriage was heaped with soft purple velvet cushions, and there

were purple satin curtains at the windows, but we pushed them to one side so we could see out. Fairy Angora sat with us, and she was almost as excited as we were when the train headed into the mountains and there was nothing but thick forest on either side of the railway track.

"Maybe we'll see a unicorn before we even get to the castle," I said hopefully.

Fairy Angora shook her head. "Don't be too disappointed if you don't see one, my darlings. They really are very rare."

We nodded, but it didn't stop us hoping...especially me. The next moment the train gave a cough and a snort, and stopped. A sign said, "Last station on the line. Alight here for Snowpine Mountain and Snowpine Castle." We grabbed our bags, and hurried out onto the platform. Lord Henry was already piling luggage onto the back of a large cart pulled by a shire horse with big brown eyes.

Diamonde and Gruella climbed out of the carriage next to ours and looked round. "There aren't any coaches to take us to the castle," Diamonde announced. "I hope no one is expecting us to WALK."

"Absolutely," Gruella said, and she sat down on a bench.

Lord Henry laughed his loud haw haw laugh. "Joking again, girls? What fun you two are! Tell you what, we'll lead the way. The rest of you can follow us. Straight up that path. The castle's right at the top. You can't miss it – not unless you're walking with your eyes shut! HAW! HAW! HAW!" And he took a twin on each arm and strode away up the hill.

"WOW!" Grace said as we stared after him. "He REALLY does know how to deal with Diamonde and Gruella!"

"This weekend's going to be FUN," Lucy agreed, and we began walking up the path.

*

Snowpine Castle wasn't beautiful, but it was very comfortable. There was a roaring fire in the huge reception hall, and loads of comfy chairs and sofas. After lunch we went to find our dormitory, and it was lovely – right up at the very top of a tower, with a fabulous view of the forest all around us. We could see the mountains stretching

into the distance, and the highest peaks were covered with snow that sparkled in the sunlight.

"Isn't it romantic?" Ellie sighed.

"If there are any unicorns we should be able to spot them from here," I said. "We should keep watch!"

"Good idea." Hannah leant against the window frame, stared out – and suddenly froze.

"OH! Isabella! LOOK!" She grabbed my arm. "Over there – can you see? WHAT IS IT?"

I leant out of the window to see what she was pointing at, and I couldn't help laughing.

"Hannah!" I said. "It's a woolly white sheep!"

Chapter Three

As Sarah and Grace began to giggle, a bell rang from down below. We hurried down the stairs together, and I saw Hannah was looking really disappointed.

"I did SO hope it was a unicorn," she said sadly as we walked into the hall. "It didn't look a BIT like a sheep to me."

"I bet other people thought it was a unicorn as well," I said comfortingly.

Diamonde heard what I said, and she gave a snooty laugh. "Goodness, Hannah! Did you think you saw a unicorn? What a wonderful imagination you have!"

"Come along, chaps – come along!" Lord Henry was waiting in the middle of the hall, holding a pile of notebooks. "Aha! My favourite twins! You can hand these out for me. Everyone else – make yourselves comfortable."

It was so funny! Diamonde and

Gruella absolutely HATE having to help (they think they're much too important) but when Lord Henry gave them the pile of notebooks they didn't say a word.

As they scurried about he went on, "On page one you'll see a list of birds, animals and insects. On the following pages are photos and descriptions. As you find each one, make a note of where you saw it, and what it was doing. Don't go too near – although none of them is dangerous. There'll be

ten tiara points for anyone who finds every bird, animal and insect on the list, and," Lord Henry winked at Fairy Angora, "an extra ten points for every whistling blue bird you see. Rare as hen's teeth, whistling blue birds. Haw! Haw! Haw! Everyone got their notebook? Excellent. Off you go –

and be sure you're back here for 5.30 sharp. We'll ring the castle bell – you'll hear that wherever you are. Oh, and there'll be another ten points for the princess who finishes first."

Sarah was looking at her list of animals. "Please, Lord Henry," she said, "there isn't a picture of a unicorn."

Lord Henry stopped looking cheerful. "No one's seen a unicorn for months, dear heart," he sighed. "We think they might have moved away to the north."

Diamonde gave a high-pitched giggle and pointed at Hannah.

"She thought she'd seen one!"

"I only wish she had," Lord Henry said sadly. "There's a family tradition that if the unicorns leave Snowpine Mountain, our castle will crumble away. Now – off you go, and do your best."

"I do feel sorry for Lord Henry," Lucy said as we walked down the path and into the forest.

"Me too," Grace agreed. "Oh! What's that?" She pointed up into the branches above our heads where a little furry animal was chattering to itself.

"It's a striped squirrel." Sarah was studying the photographs in her notebook. "I'll tick it off."

*

It was a lovely afternoon. We wandered in and out of the trees, and we saw lots more squirrels and sheep. And there were rabbits and deer and all kinds of birds and butterflies – it was wonderful! The sun shone through the leaves and dappled the grass, and every so often we'd find patches of sky-blue flowers that smelt heavenly.

"Isn't this FABULOUS?" Ellie said as we came out of the trees and found ourselves near the top of Snowpine Mountain. "Oh – look! Isn't that a silver eagle? Can you see? Up near that rock!"

"Hurrah!" Sarah waved her notebook triumphantly. "That's the last thing on our list! Ten tiara points for us!"

"I'll write down where we saw it," Hannah said. "Oops – I've broken my pencil. Isabella, can I borrow yours?"

I didn't answer. I was staring and staring at a clump of tall dark pine trees not far below where we were standing. Had I seen something moving? Something white? My

eyes actually hurt, I was staring so hard.

And then I saw it...and I began to tremble. The most exquisite unicorn walked out from the trees, across a grassy clearing, and was lost again in the forest. Close beside it ran a tiny snow-white foal.

I was so amazed I could hardly breathe.

"Wasn't that the most beautiful thing you've ever seen?" Sarah whispered.

Grace nodded, and Ellie rubbed her eyes.

"The baby didn't even have a horn, it was so tiny," Lucy said wonderingly. "It was MAGIC!"

Chapter Four

"Won't Lord Henry be pleased?" Hannah said as we made our way back down the mountain.

"Pleased about WHAT?" a loud voice asked, and Diamonde and Gruella appeared from the other direction.

"We saw a unicorn!" I was so excited I couldn't stop myself.

"We actually did! AND it had a foal running beside it!"

Diamonde looked at Gruella, her eyebrows raised. "Isabella's seeing things now," she said. "Perhaps we should tell Fairy Angora she's been in the sun too long."

Gruella giggled.

"But we really DID see them!" I protested.

"Don't even bother, Isabella," Hannah told me. "We know what we saw. It doesn't matter if they don't believe us."

"OOOOH!" Diamonde sneered. "Well, WE'VE seen all the animals on our list, and we've seen FIVE whistling blue birds, haven't we, Gruella?"

Gruella hesitated. "Was it five?" she asked doubtfully.

"Yes," Diamonde said firmly. "It was. And now we're going back to the castle to collect LOADS of tiara points!"

As they stamped away I noticed that Gruella was limping, and a moment later she stopped.

"Wait a minute, Diamonde," she said. "My foot really hurts. There's a stream over there – maybe I could wash it—"

"Don't be silly, Gruella!" Diamonde snapped. "We want to be first back, don't we?"

"But it hurts a lot!" Gruella wailed, and she sat down on the tree trunk.

"Well, I'm not waiting for you! You can come back with the loopy Lilies." Diamonde made a face, and set off along the path as fast as she could go.

Gruella sighed, and pulled off her shoe. Her foot looked very red and swollen, and there was an enormous blister on her heel.

"POOR Gruella!" Lucy said. "That looks really sore!"

"It is." Gruella bit her lip. "I got a stone in my shoe, and Diamonde wouldn't stop. And then it got worse and worse and worse and now it's AGONY."

"Here –" Ellie pulled a spotless hankie out of her pocket. "Maybe we could use this as a bandage."

"Wouldn't it be better if it was wet?" I asked. Ellie nodded and handed me the hankie, and I ran towards the stream. The water was icy cold and very clear, and as I knelt down I could see every pebble at the bottom.

I was wringing the hankie out when something made me look up

– and there, on the other side of
the stream, was the baby unicorn.

He gazed at me with his huge dark eyes, and I froze. Then he gave a funny little whinny, tossed his head, and trotted into the forest. Just before he vanished among the trees I saw that although he was snow-white from head to tail, there was a strange mark on his neck – almost like a letter S.

Chapter Five

It was odd. I didn't feel excited – but I did feel SO honoured, and proud. And – I'm not quite sure why – when I got back to the others I didn't tell them what I'd seen. I watched Lucy wash Gruella's foot, and then we all helped her hobble back to the castle. We were almost there when the bell began to ring.

"There's Fairy Angora by the gate," Hannah said. "Keep going, Gruella – you'll be fine as soon as she treats your poor foot. You'll be running about in no time!"

Fairy Angora came hurrying towards us, looking anxious.

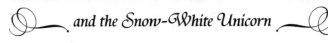

"You poor petal, Gruella!" she cooed. "Diamonde said you'd hurt your foot. Wasn't it so sweet of her to hurry on ahead to warn me? I gave her an extra five tiara points for being so thoughtful."

Hannah and I looked at each other, but we didn't say anything. Gruella's face went bright red. "Diamonde only ran on ahead so she'd be first back at the castle," she said crossly. "She wouldn't wait for me, would she, Isabella?"

"Erm..." I began. I didn't want to tell tales, but I didn't want to defend Diamonde either. "Erm...she was in rather a hurry."

Fairy Angora put her arm round Gruella. "Come inside, angel. Everyone else is back, and supper's almost ready. I'll see to your foot after supper, and then you'll be fine."

We went into the hall, and found the other Pearl Palace princesses settled on chairs or sofas. Lord Henry was sitting in a tall chair at the head of a long wooden table.

"Ho ho!" He clapped his hands when he saw us come in. "Come along and make yourselves comfortable!" Diamonde was sitting beside him looking very pleased with herself, and when Gruella came limping in Lord Henry called her over to the empty chair on his other side.

"Gruella!" Diamonde stood up and waved to her twin. "I've told Lord Henry how well we did and how we saw five whistling blue birds! He was SO impressed he couldn't say a word! He's going to tell everyone how many tiara points we've got because I just know we've got LOADS more than everyone else." And she sat back down beside Lord Henry with a huge self-satisfied smile.

As Gruella sat down on his other side I couldn't help wondering what Lord Henry was thinking. There was SUCH an odd expression on his face – but all he

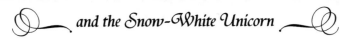

said was, "You're quite right, Princess Diamonde. In fact, I have an important announcement to make."

"Thank you SO very much," Diamonde simpered. "We did try SO hard." She glanced slyly at me. "Of course I wasn't as lucky as Isabella and the others in Lily Room. Isabella says they actually saw a unicorn!"

Everyone turned to look at me, and I couldn't help blushing as I stood up.

"I did see a unicorn," I said. "We all did. And we saw a baby unicorn as well."

59

There was a silence, and then Lord Henry got up from his chair.

"Princess Isabella," he said, and he sounded very serious. "Please tell me the truth. Did you REALLY see a unicorn and her foal? Or are you telling lies, like the Princesses Diamonde and Gruella?"

You could have heard a pin drop. Gruella's eyes popped, and Diamonde's mouth hung open... until she began to scream.

"I NEVER tell lies! I DID see five whistling blue birds! I did, I did, I DID! Tell him, Gruella! TELL—"

Lord Henry held up his hand. "Silence!" he said, and there was something so steely about his voice that Diamonde stopped mid-shriek.

"There are NO whistling blue birds," he went on. "Do you hear me? There are no such things. I made them up as a joke – and now, twins, it seems the joke is on you."

As Diamonde and Gruella sank down in their chairs, Lord Henry turned to me. "I'll ask you one more time, Princess Isabella – what did you see?"

"We saw a unicorn." I spoke as clearly as I could. "We saw a unicorn, and a little one beside her. They were near the top of the mountain, among the tall pine trees, in a grassy clearing."

I took a deep breath. "And then,

later on, I saw the baby down by the stream. He had a strange mark on his neck—"

"Wait!" Lord Henry strode across the hall, his eyes shining.

"Say that again! He had a mark on his neck? Are you sure?"

I nodded. "It looked just like a letter S."

I thought Lord Henry was going to burst into song, he looked so happy. He grabbed my hands, and whirled me round the hall until I was giddy. "You DID see them! Nobody could make that up – it's the secret mark of the Snowpine unicorns! Princess Isabella – this calls for a celebration! Tonight we'll have a party you'll never forget. Fairy Angora, you'll help me, won't you?"

Chapter Six

Fairy Angora isn't always brilliant at magic, but at Snowpine Castle she was absolutely wonderful. She waved her wand, and sparkling stars floated down and shone brightly from the huge beams that stretched across the hall. Silver bells swung from the ceiling, and pink and silver ribbons looped over the walls and tied themselves into bows. Music began to play, very softly at first, but when Lord Henry opened the great castle door six musicians came marching in dressed

in silver satin and pink velvet.

"I wish I'd brought one of my ball dresses with me," Grace said wistfully as the music grew louder and louder.

"Ballgowns?" Lord Henry's face was one big happy smile. "NO problem. Come with me, princesses…" and he led us up to a row of simply massive wardrobes in one of the castle rooms. "Do help yourselves!"

We opened the doors of the nearest wardrobe...and gasped in wonder. It was STUFFED with the most gorgeous dresses. We each chose one, and Fairy Angora waved her wand...and they fitted us perfectly!

We rustled our way down the grand staircase, and a trumpeter sounded a fanfare as we reached the hall. Then the music began to

play again, and we danced and we danced until the moon was high in the sky. It was utterly UTTERLY glorious.

At last the magic stars began to fade, the musicians bowed and disappeared, and Fairy Angora told us it was time for bed. We thanked Lord Henry for the most wonderful time, and climbed slowly up to our tower bedroom, yawning as we went.

Ellie and Grace flopped onto their beds, but I went to the window to look at the real stars...and there, down below, were the two unicorns. I watched as they walked gracefully to the end of the drawbridge and stopped for a long minute before moving away again. Lord Henry was leaning against the open castle door, gazing at them happily.

"I think today was one of the best days in my whole life," Lucy said sleepily as I came away from the window. "Lovely dancing, and magical unicorns..."

"And very VERY lovely friends,"
I said as I climbed into bed.

And I meant it.

I've got the best friends ever...
Hannah, Ellie, Lucy, Sarah,
Grace...and YOU.

What happens next?
Find out in

Princess Lucy

and the **Precious Puppy**

Hi! I'm Princess Lucy, and I'm one
of the Lily Room princesses - and
I'm so very pleased you're here too.
You really are a Perfect Princess -
not like Diamonde and Gruella.
I'm lucky I've got you as a friend -
and I know Hannah, Isabella, Grace,
Ellie and Sarah think so too.
And I REALLY need my friends
when it's time for Sports Day...

Look out for

Princess Parade

with Princess Hannah and Princess Lucy
ISBN 978 1 84616 504 7

And look out for the Daffodil Room princesses in
the Tiara Club at Emerald Castle:

Win a Tiara Club
Perfect Princess Prize!

Look for the secret word in mirror writing that is
hidden in a tiara in each of the Tiara Club books.
Each book has one word. Put together the six words
from books **19** to **24** to make a special Perfect
Princess sentence, then send it to us together with
20 words or more on why you like the Tiara Club
books. Each month, we will put the correct entries
in a draw and one lucky reader will receive a magical
Perfect Princess prize!

Send your Perfect Princess sentence,
at least 20 words on why you like the Tiara Club,
your name and your address on a postcard to:
THE TIARA CLUB COMPETITION,
Orchard Books, 338 Euston Road,
London, NW1 3BH

Australian readers should write to:
Hachette Children's Books,
Level 17/207 Kent Street, Sydney, NSW 2000.

Only one entry per child.
Final draw: 30 September 2008

By Vivian French
Illustrated by Sarah Gibb

The Tiara Club

The Tiara Club at Silver Towers

The Tiara Club at Ruby Mansions

The Tiara Club at Pearl Palace

PRINCESS HANNAH AND THE **LITTLE BLACK KITTEN**	ISBN	978 1 84616 498 9
PRINCESS ISABELLA AND THE **SNOW-WHITE UNICORN**	ISBN	978 1 84616 499 6
PRINCESS LUCY AND THE **PRECIOUS PUPPY**	ISBN	978 1 84616 500 9
PRINCESS GRACE AND THE **GOLDEN NIGHTINGALE**	ISBN	978 1 84616 501 6
PRINCESS ELLIE AND THE **ENCHANTED FAWN**	ISBN	978 1 84616 502 3
PRINCESS SARAH AND THE **SILVER SWAN**	ISBN	978 1 84616 503 0
BUTTERFLY BALL	ISBN	978 1 84616 470 5
CHRISTMAS WONDERLAND	ISBN	978 1 84616 296 1
PRINCESS PARADE	ISBN	978 1 84616 504 7

All priced at £3.99.
Butterfly Ball, Christmas Wonderland and *Princess Parade* are priced at £5.99.
The Tiara Club books are available from all good bookshops, or can be ordered
direct from the publisher: Orchard Books, PO BOX 29, Douglas IM99 1BQ.
Credit card orders please telephone 01624 836000
or fax 01624 837033 or visit our website: www.orchardbooks.co.uk
or e-mail: bookshop@enterprise.net for details.

To order please quote title, author and ISBN and your full name and address.
Cheques and postal orders should be made payable to 'Bookpost plc.'
Postage and packing is FREE within the UK
(overseas customers should add £2.00 per book).

Prices and availability are subject to change.

Check out

The Tiara Club

website at:

www.tiaraclub.co.uk

You'll find Perfect Princess games and fun things to do, as well as news on the Tiara Club and all your favourite princesses!